MW01129887

A Small Treasury
of

CHRISTMAS

Poems and Prayers

Illustrated by Susan Spellman

A Small Treasury of CHRISTMAS

Poems and Prayers

Illustrated by Susan Spellman

BOYDS MILLS PRESS

Published by Bell Books
Boyds Mills Press, Inc.
A Highlights Company
815 Church Street
Honesdale, Pennsylvania 18431
Printed in Mexico

Publisher Cataloging-in-Publication Data
A small treasury of Christmas poems and prayers / illustrated by Susan Spellman.—1st ed.
[32]p. : col.ill. ; cm.
Summary : A collection of verse celebrating Christmas.
ISBN 1-56397-680-3
1. Christmas—Children's poetry. 2. Prayers—Children's literature.
[1. Christmas—Poetry. 2. Prayers.] I. Spellman, Susan, ill. II. Title.
808.8 /033—dc20 1997 AC CIP
Library of Congress Catalog Card Number 97-70362

First edition, 1997
Book designed by Tim Gillner
The text of this book is set in 14-point Minion.
The illustrations are done in colored pencil.

10 9 8 7 6 5 4 3 2 1

Acknowledgements:

Every possible effort has been made to trace the ownership of each poem included in *A Small Treasury of Christmas Poems and Prayers.* If any errors or omissions have occured, corrections will be made in subsequent printings, provided the publisher is notified of their existence.

Permission to reprint copyrighted poems is gratefully acknowledged to the following:

Aileen Fisher for "In December" by Aileen Fisher from *Highlights for Children.* Copyright © 1967 by Aileen Fisher.

Margaret K. McElderry Books, an imprint of Simon & Schuster Children's Publishing Division, for "Christmas Kaleidoscope" from *The Forgetful Wishing Well* by X. J. Kennedy. Copyright © 1985 by X. J. Kennedy.

Elizabeth Roach for "Christmas" from *Around and About* by Marchette Chute. Copyright © 1957 by E. P. Dutton. Copyright © renewed in 1984 by Marchette Chute.

CONTENTS

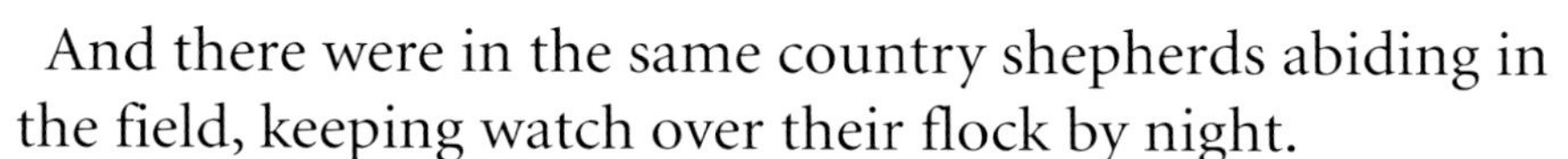

And there were in the same country shepherds abiding in the field, keeping watch over their flock by night.

And, lo, the angel of the Lord came upon them, and the glory of the Lord shone about them, and they were sore afraid.

And the angel said unto them, Fear not, for behold I bring you good tidings of great joy, which shall be to all people.

For unto you is born this day in the city of David a Saviour, which is Christ the Lord.

And this shall be a sign unto you. Ye shall find the babe wrapped in swaddling clothes, lying in a manger.

And suddenly there was with the angel a multitude of heavenly host praising God, and saying,

Glory to God in the highest, and on earth peace, goodwill toward men.

And it came to pass, as the angels were gone away from them into heaven, the shepherds said one to another, Let us now go even unto Bethlehem, and see this thing which is come to pass, which the Lord hath made known unto us.

And they came with haste, and found Mary and Joseph, and the babe lying in a manger.

And when they had seen it, they made known abroad the saying which was told them concerning the child.

And all they that heard it wondered at those things which were told them by the shepherds.

Luke 2:8-18

Our Christmas Candle

Our Christmas candle,
Warm and bright,
Stands for the star
Whose blessed light
Shone on the Magi
And guided them
Over the desert
To Bethlehem.
So every year
In the month of December
While candles glow,
We shall remember
The star in the east
And the Kings who came
To worship the Savior
And bless His name.

—Rowena Cheney

Christmas Bells

I heard the bells on Christmas Day
Their old, familiar carols play,
And wild and sweet the words repeat
Of peace on earth, goodwill to men!

And thought how, as the day had come,
The belfries of all Christendom
Had rolled along the unbroken song
Of peace on earth, goodwill to men.

And in despair I bowed my head;
"There is no peace on earth," I said;
"For hate is strong and mocks the song
Of peace on earth, goodwill to men!"

Then pealed the bells more loud and deep:
"God is not dead, nor doth He sleep!
The wrong shall fail, the right prevail,
With peace on earth, goodwill to men!"

Till ringing, singing on its way
The world revolved from night to day,
A voice, a chime, a chant sublime,
Of peace on earth, goodwill to men.

—Henry Wadsworth Longfellow

Sing Hey!

Sing hey! Sing hey!
For Christmas Day
Twine mistletoe and holly.
For friendship glows
In winter snows,
And so let's all be jolly.

—Anonymous

As Joseph Was A-Walking

As Joseph was a-walking,
He heard an angel sing,
"This night shall be the birthnight
Of Christ our heavenly King.

"His birthbed shall be neither
In housen nor in hall,
Nor in the place of Paradise,
But in the oxen's stall.

"He neither shall be rocked
In silver nor in gold,
But in the wooden manger
That lieth in the mold."

As Joseph was a-walking,
Thus did the angel sing,
And Mary's Son at midnight,
Was born to be our King.

Then be you glad, good people;
At this time of the year:
And light you up your candles
For His star it shineth clear.

—Anonymous

Ring Me A Rhyme

Ring me a rhyme
of Christmastime,
a farmhouse and a stable,
where for one strange
and mystic night
the animals were able
to speak with human
voice and welcome
one small human stranger—
an Infant sent
from Heaven-high,
a Baby in a manger.

—Ivy O. Eastwick

My Gift

What can I give Him,
Poor as I am?
If I were a shepherd,
I would give Him a lamb.
If I were a wise man,
I would do my part.
But what can I give Him?
I will give my heart.

—Christina Rossetti

December

Dimmest and brightest month am I;
My short days end, my lengthening days begin;
What matters more or less sun in the sky,
When all is sun within?

Ivy and privet dark as night,
I weave with hips and haws a cheerful show,
And holly for a beauty and delight,
And milky mistletoe.

While high above them all I set
Yew twigs and Christmas roses pure and pale;
Then Spring her snowdrop and her violet
May keep, so sweet and frail;

May keep each merry singing bird,
Of all her happy birds that singing build:
For I've a carol which some shepherds heard
Once in a wintry field.

—Christina Rossetti

A Little Child

A little Child,
A shining star.
A stable rude,
The door ajar.

Yet in that place,
So crude, forlorn,
The hope of all
The world was born.

—Anonymous

Hark! The Christmas Bells Are Ringing

Hark! The Christmas bells are ringing
  Ringing through the frosty air—
Happiness to each one bringing,
  And release from toil and care.

How the merry peal is swelling
  From the gray, old crumbling tower,
To the simplest creature telling
  Of almighty love and power.

Neighbors shaking hands and greeting,
  No one sorrowing, no one sad,
Children, loving parents meeting,
  Young and old alike are glad.

Then while Christmas bells are ringing,
  Rich and poor, your voices raise,
And—your simple carol singing—
  Waft to heaven your grateful praise.

—Anonymous

God Bless the Master of this House

God bless the master of this house,
Likewise the mistress, too,
And all the little children
That 'round the table go;

And all your kin and kinsmen
That dwell both far and near.
I wish you a Merry Christmas
And a Happy New Year.

—Anonymous

Long, Long Ago

Winds through the olive trees
  Softly did blow,
'Round little Bethlehem,
  Long, long ago.

Sheep on the hillside lay
  Whiter than snow.
Shepherds were watching them,
  Long, long ago.

Then from the happy sky,
  Angels bent low,
Singing their songs of joy,
  Long, long ago.

For in a manger bed,
  Cradled we know,
Christ came to Bethlehem
  Long, long ago.

—Anonymous

The Lamb

Little Lamb, who made thee?
Dost thou know who made thee?
Gave thee life, and bade thee feed
By the stream and o'er the mead;
Gave thee clothing of delight,
Softest clothing a woolly, bright;
Gave thee such a tender voice,
Making all the vales rejoice?
Little Lamb, who made thee?
Dost thou know who made thee?

Little Lamb, I'll tell thee;
Little Lamb, I'll tell thee.
He is called by thy name,
For he calls himself a Lamb.
He is meek and He is mild;
He became a little child.
I a child, and thou a Lamb,
We are called by His Name.
Little Lamb, God bless thee!
Little Lamb, God bless thee!

—William Blake

In December

Everyone is merry now.
Go walking down the street,
And twinkly eyes and winkly eyes
Are all the eyes you meet.

Everyone is eager now
To shop and trim a tree,
And knowing smiles and glowing smiles
Are all the smiles you see.

Everyone is jolly now,
This tingly-jingly season.
And only cats and puppy-dogs
Can't understand the reason!

—Aileen Fisher

The Joy of Giving

Somehow, not only for Christmas
But all the long year through,
The joy that you give to others
Is the joy that comes back to you;
And the more you spend in blessing
The poor and lonely and sad,
The more of your heart's possessing
Returns to make you glad.

—John Greenleaf Whittier

The Bells

Hear the sledges with the bells,
Silver bells!
What a world of merriment their
melody foretells!
How they tinkle, tinkle, tinkle,
In the icy air of night!
While the stars that oversprinkle
All the heavens seem to twinkle
With a crystalline delight;
Keeping time, time, time,
In a sort of Runic rhyme,
To the tintinnabulation that so
musically wells
From the bells, bells, bells, bells,
Bells, bells, bells—
From the jingling and the
tinkling of the bells.

—Edgar Allan Poe

IN A FAIR STABLE

Mary on the donkey
sings a sad little song;
the road has been a weary one,
far too long—
"Overhead the gray sky,
gray since morn,
where, oh where
shall my Babe be born?"

Mary in the meadow
sings a sad little tune;
overhead is one star
and the pale winter moon—
"Snow on the holly,
ice on the thorn,
where, oh where
shall my Babe be born?"

All around, the thorn trees
wear garments of snow;
over all, the moonlight
sheds a cold, green glow.
Mary needs a room where
her Babe may be born,
out of the wintry fields,
away from the storm.

"Here, Mary! Here, Mary,"
Dove's voice coos.
"Here, Mary! Here, Mary,"
Oxen lows.
"Here, Mary! Here, Mary,"
Gray donkey brays.
And, "Here is a stable, Mary,"
Joseph says.

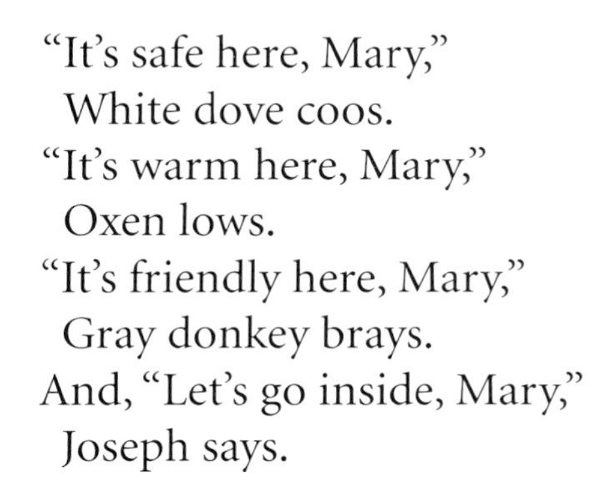

"It's safe here, Mary,"
 White dove coos.
"It's warm here, Mary,"
 Oxen lows.
"It's friendly here, Mary,"
 Gray donkey brays.
And, "Let's go inside, Mary,"
 Joseph says.

But almost before
he has finished these words,
out of the sky
like white star-birds
the angels descended,
shining and bright,
filling the stable
with glorious light.
"Here, Mary," voices
 of Cherubim rang.
"Here, Mary! Here, Mary,"
 Seraphim sang.

"Hail, Mary. Sweet, Mary,
full of God's grace,
a stable, a stable,
shall be His birthplace.
Princes choose palace
and manor and hall,
but He Who is King
and the Lord of us all,
chooses for birthplace
a manger this night,
surrounded by love
and protected by light."

Never was stable
more radiant, more fair;
songs of thanksgiving
and praise filled the air.
So, out of the meadow,
away from the storm,
in a fair stable
was Mary's Son born.

—Ivy O. Eastwick

CHRISTMAS

My Goodness, my goodness,
It's Christmas again.
The bells are all ringing.
I do not know when
I've been so excited.
The tree is all fixed,
The candles are lighted,
The pudding is mixed.

The wreath's on the door
And the carols are sung,
The presents are wrapped
And the holly is hung.
The turkey is sitting
All safe in its pan,
And I am behaving
As calm as I can.

—Marchette Chute

Christmas Kaleidoscope

Chock-full boxes, packages—
squeeze 'em, feel sharp edges!
From candycaned
evergreen
a tinfoil
rainfall
dangles.

Cold-tongued bells are tolling,
tolling, Hark, the herald
angels sing
Christ the King!
Earth's
rebirth
is caroled.

Sheep and ox guard manger
Magi offer gifts.
Down through white
silent night
slow
snow
sifts.

—X. J. Kennedy

While Shepherds Watched Their Flocks by Night

While shepherds watched their flocks by night
All seated on the ground,
The angel of the Lord came down,
And glory shone around.

"Fear not," said he, for mighty dread
Had seized their troubled mind;
"Glad tidings of great joy I bring
To you and all mankind.

"To you, in David's town, this day
Is born, of David's line,
The Saviour, who is Christ the Lord,
And this shall be the sign:

"The heavenly Babe you there shall find
To human view displayed,
All meanly wrapped in swaddling bands,
And in a manger laid."

Thus spake the seraph; and forthwith
Appeared a shining throng
Of angels, praising God, who thus
Addressed their joyful song:

"All glory be to God on high,
And to the earth be peace;
Goodwill henceforth from Heaven to men
Begin and never cease."

—Nahum Tate

CRADLE HYMN

Away in a manger, no crib for a bed
The little Lord Jesus laid down His sweet head.
The stars in the bright sky looked down where He lay—
The little Lord Jesus asleep on the hay.

The cattle are lowing, the baby awakes,
But little Lord Jesus, no crying he makes.
I love thee, Lord Jesus! Look down from the sky,
And stay by my cradle till morning is nigh.

—Martin Luther

From Heaven High

From Heaven high I come to you;
I bring you news both good and true.
Glad tidings of great joy I bring;
To you is born this night a King.

To you is born this night a Child,
Of Virgin Mary meek and mild;
A Child so blessed, and full of love,
Sent for your joy from Heaven above.

—Martin Luther

Father, We Thank Thee for the Night

Father, we thank thee for the night.
Keep us safe till morning light,
As the shepherd in his fold
Keeps his sheep from harm and cold.
Bless all friends to us so dear,
Father, Mother, and all here,
And may Thy little children be
Ever very near to Thee.

—Anonymous

CHRISTMAS PRAYER

O God, thank You for sending Your only Son into the world as an example to us. Help us to follow in His footsteps, and like Him to grow in wisdom and in stature and in favor with You, as we celebrate His birth year after year. Amen.

—Adelyn Jackson Richards

The Virgin's Slumber Song

Shoon-a-shoon,
I sing no psalm
Little Man,
Although I am
Out of David's
House and Clan.
Shoon-a-shoon
I sing no psalm.

(*Hush-a-hoo,*
Blowing of pine;
Hush-a-hoo,
Lowing of kine:
Hush-a-hoo,
Though even in sleep,
His ear can hear
The shamrock's creep.)

O'er and o'er
And under all,
Every star
Is now a ball,
For Your little
Hands that are
O'er and o'er
And under all.

(*Hush-a-hoo,*
Whirring of wings;
Hush-a-hoo,
Stirring of strings:
Hush-a-hoo,
Though in slumber deep
His ear can hear
My Song of Sleep.)

—Francis Carlin

Goodnight

Goodnight! Goodnight!
Far flies the light:
  But still God's love
  Shall flame above,
Making all bright.
Goodnight! Goodnight!

—Victor Hugo